Thumbelina

All thanks to my beloved mother,
who always keeps a beautiful
garden. Time and again she
read H. C. A. to my brother
and me. — X. G. K.

For my daughter, Violette.
I love you forever and always. — C. G.

Barefoot Books
2067 Massachusetts Ave
Cambridge, MA 02140

Barefoot Books
29/30 Fitzroy Square
London, W1T 6LQ

Adapted from the fairy tale by Hans Christian Andersen
Text adaptation copyright © 2016 by Xanthe Gresham Knight
Illustrations by Charlotte Gastaut
Illustrations copyright © 2011 by Éditions Flammarion
The moral rights of Xanthe Gresham Knight
and Charlotte Gastaut have been asserted

First published in France by Éditions Flammarion in 2011
First published in the United States of America by Barefoot Books, Inc and in
Great Britain by Barefoot Books, Ltd in 2016

Graphic design by Sarah Soldano, Barefoot Books
English-language edition edited by KMJ DePalma, Barefoot Books
Reproduction by B & P International, Hong Kong
Printed in China on 100% acid-free paper
This book was typeset in Janson, Albemarle and Albemarle Swash

ISBN 978-1-78285-276-6

Library of Congress Cataloging-in-Publication Data
is available upon request

British Cataloguing-in-Publication Data: a catalogue record for this book
is available from the British Library

1 3 5 7 9 8 6 4 2

Thumbelina

Retold by Xanthe Gresham Knight
Illustrated by Charlotte Gastaut

Barefoot Books
step inside a story

Contents

CHAPTER ONE

A Girl Named Thumbelina

There was once a mother who didn't have a child. How she wanted one! She told the swallows in the sky, "I want a child." She told the flowers in her garden, "I want a child." She told the fish in the river, "I want a child."

She said it so often the birds sang, the flowers nodded, the fish mouthed, *She wants a child. She wants a child. She wants a child.*

Early one morning, an old woman came hobbling down the road with a basketful of seeds. As she listened to the birds, the flowers and the fish, her ears bristled like a field of wheat. She knocked on Mother's door.

"You want a child?" asked the old woman.

"Yes, please!"

"Take a pocket of air, a pinch of sun, a peck of rainbow, plant them and you'll get your child."

"But that's impossible!" wept Mother. At this the old woman laughed such a long *tee heeeeeee* she had to lean against the wall to stop from falling over.

"It's already done!" she said, pushing a seed into Mother's hand.

Eyes shining, Mother planted the seed in a pot, sat with her hands on the table, her chin on her hands, and watched.

For one hour, two hours, nothing happened. Three hours, four hours, nothing happened — then in a blink, *whoosh!*

A stalk pushed through the soil. At the end of the stalk was a yellow bud. The bud swelled and swelled until it was a bell-shaped flower. It opened. And there, balanced on the soft petals was a tiny, tiny, wee little girl. A girl like there has never been before and never will be again.

She was no taller than Mother's thumb, with eyes as brown as berries, lips as red as cherries and cheeks an apple-blossom pink. She blinked, shook her ink-black hair and dove straight into the bowl of flowers. They scattered and made a swimming pool!

"Well!" said the tiny, tiny, wee little girl's mother. "You are a real Thumbelina!"

At this, the girl began to sing,

> I am Thumb, I am Thumble, I'm Thumbelina!
> I can tumble in here with a SPLASH,
> I can kick with each toe,
> I can swim quick, quick, slow,
> It's me, Thumbelina, HELLO!

She frolicked in the water like a lark in a birdbath until *yawn, stre-e-e-tch, kerdung* — her head fell on her chest and she was asleep.

Ever so carefully, Mother picked up tiny Thumbelina and placed her in a little bed. It was made from half a walnut shell lined with moss, with violets for a mattress and a rose-petal blanket.

CHAPTER TWO

Kidnapped!

At first light, Thumbelina leapt out of bed and onto the table.

I am Thumb, I am Thumble, I'm Thumbelina!
I can drum with my feet, I can bow,
I can stamp, I can bounce,
I can flick, I can flounce,
What can Thumbelina do now?

"You could get dressed!" said Mother. "But what will you wear? Hmm. Let's see!"

Mother plucked some silken petals from flowers in the bowl, found a strand of gossamer left by a spider and, last of all, picked out a needle so tiny she couldn't thread it. "I can do it!" clapped Thumbelina. And she did.

Then Mother taught her how to sew. Scarcely bigger than the needle, Thumbelina soon found a rhythm in her stitching. "In and out and pull it through, in and out and pull it through, and tie a little knot. Snap!" She bit the thread. Thumbelina sewed skirts of leaves, jackets of cobwebs and shoes of silver fish scales. At night, she slept in a simple dress she'd made from the grey of one of Mother's handkerchiefs.

When Thumbelina wasn't sewing with Mother, she spent her time somersaulting, walking on her hands and singing at the top of her voice until *yawn, stre-e-e-tch, kerdung* — she fell asleep. Every night she slept soundly tucked up in her little walnut shell.

One night, after the moon had risen and the crickets had fallen silent, a small explosion leapt out of the reeds beside the stream. A toad came walloping up the path and sprang onto the window ledge. Squeezing her lumpy green body through the gap in the window, she plopped onto the table and looked at Thumbelina. *Krrroooooak.*

A black strand of hair fell across Thumbelina's pink cheek.

"What a pretty, plump insect!" said the toad, batting her fat eye and swelling her fat chest. "A perfect dish for my son's birthday banquet."

The toad scooped up the walnut bed and leapt back out the window. She squelched back to the marsh and dropped Thumbelina beside her snake-eyed son. "See what a treat I've found for your special day!"

Toad Son let out a long, rusty warble like a broken musical box. *Ker, ker, ker, krrroooooak!*

"Shhh! We don't want to wake the delicacy until the party is ready. Then you can eat it alive!"

Toad Mother swam out to a lily pad in the middle of the stream with Thumbelina still in her walnut shell and left her there, a sleeping prisoner surrounded by water.

Then she and Toad Son began to prepare for

the party. Toad Mother made a marsh palace of slime. Toad Son collected a banquet; again and again he stuck out his sticky tongue to catch insects, all the while singing:

> **Yum, yum! White flies and fruit flies**
> **   and small white grubs,**
> **Slurp, slurp! Spiders and gliders,**
> **   soft slugs and bugs,**
> **Crunch, crunch! Crispy green crickets,**
> **   lice and small mice,**
> **Croak, croak! Slimy, fat maggots**
> **   and aphids are nice . . .**

Finally, when there were countless dock leaves piled high with delicacies and the marsh palace was dripping with swamp flowers, everything was ready and the guests began to arrive.

A short distance away, on her leaf, Thumbelina woke up, opening her eyes to the widest thing she'd ever seen — the sky. Her stomach was turning with the rocking of the stream beneath the leaf. She climbed out of her walnut shell, then screamed, because two slimy green heads popped up from the stream. *Splash*. Her safe, warm walnut shell fell into the water.

"It's all yours!" trilled Toad Mother.

"Soft yet crunchy, munchy, munchy!" creaked Toad Son.

But when he leapt onto the leaf, Thumbelina kicked and flipped and fought him off. "Party game!" exclaimed Toad Son, and let her push him back into the stream. Then he hopped onto the leaf again and again and again.

"Stop!" Thumbelina shouted over the sound of splashing water. "Leave me alone!"

Now, the fish beneath the water and the birds in the air were watching. They thought it wouldn't do at all for Thumbelina, as light as a feather, as bright as a dewdrop, to be eaten by a greedy old toad! With one mind, the glittering fish began to gnaw and gnaw at the stalk of the lily pad with their strong teeth. The birds cawed and cawed, "Faster, faster!" Thumbelina reached below the water and yanked the stalk with all her might, as if she were ripping out a stubborn seam. The stalk snapped.

"Thank you!" she called to the birds and the fish as she spun away downstream.

Chapter Three

The Beetle

As Thumbelina floated, her mouth dropped open. The sky was so blue, the bird song so pure, the water so bright! She lay flat on her back and drifted . . . until a pink butterfly fluttered above her head. Thumbelina took a thread from her dress and tied it to him gently with a bow she could undo with one tug.

Delighted, the butterfly pulled her along the stream. Fast, fast, faster went Thumbelina until the trees blurred, the light sparkled and the water around her went white. Her heart pounded, but the wind in her hair made her feel free.

> I am Thumb, I am Thumble, I'm Thumbelina!
> I can float, I can skim, I can SING,
> I am water and whizz,
> I am froth, I am fizz,
> I am Thumbleen-ishka-kin-KIN!

Just then Thumbelina heard a great buzzing and a roaring above her head. Something banged into her. Something with legs and claws and probes. She had no time to react before the creature grabbed hold of her and flew up into the air. It was a beetle.

All Thumbelina could think about was the butterfly. It must still be flying downstream. Attached to the lily leaf, he would never get free, and without food he would surely die.

The beetle didn't care about a butterfly.

Bzzzrrrrr! He took his prize to the branch of a great oak tree and set her down in a crawling heap of beetles.

"Gather, gather!" he called, pumping his wings and waving his antennae. "One of the giants but tiny, so tiny! She's only as big as my wing. Isn't she something?"

All the other beetles began to cluster around Thumbelina, prodding her with their claws.

"What is she?"

"She's so ugly!"

"Where are her other legs?"

"Why is she so soft, so skinny?"

"She's got no feelers!"

"She must be very stupid!"

Thumbelina's cheeks flushed with anger. "Hey!" she cried. "I'm not ugly. I'm not stupid. I'm Thumbelina!"

The beetle began to think he had made a mistake. He thought Thumbelina was lovely, but the comments of his beetle brothers put him off. He carried her down from the tree, dropped her in a flower and *bzzzrrrrr!* flew away.

CHAPTER FOUR

Mrs. Mouse and Mr. Mole

Mother called for Thumbelina all the next day until she saw a pink butterfly tied to a lily leaf by grey thread. She recognized the thread from Thumbelina's dress. Mother waded into the river, gave the bow of thread a little tug and set the butterfly free. As it landed on a flower, Mother wiped her eyes and walked home.

But Thumbelina hadn't drowned. Far away she was running through the meadows, lost in the scent of wildflowers and the sound of birdsong. For food she ate nectar; for drink, raindrops. She never stopped dancing, but now she did it quietly, secretly, to avoid dangerous attention. She learned how to melt into moss, sink into sunlight and fade into flowers. At night she rolled herself in fat leaves, looked at the stars and remained free.

But as the earth turned, the days got shorter and colder. Leaves fell from trees and petals fell from flowers. The rain came, the winds blew and the skies went quiet. The birds had flown away with the sun. Thumbelina's clothes were rags, her hair was frozen, and when she tried to wrap herself in a dry leaf it cracked and split. Then it snowed. Every snowflake was like a basket of snow falling on her head. Only as high as a thumb, she was afraid she would drown in a blanket of thick, cold, silent white.

Walking through the fields one day, dodging stumps of short, dry, sharp wheat, Thumbelina saw a little door in the stubble. It was made of polished wood with a shiny knocker. She tapped and heard scuffling. The door was opened by a plump little field mouse wearing a clean, smooth apron. She had sharp, twinkly eyes and spectacles on the end of her black, shiny nose.

"I'm so cold and so hungry. Can you help?" asked Thumbelina.

The mouse removed her spectacles and folded up her apron. She put her head to one side, twitched her whiskers, then threw her tiny paws around Thumbelina's waist and pulled her in.

"Of course, my dear! Come inside, quick, quick! You can stay here awhile," she whiffled. "I don't get around like I used to. You could help me brush-a brush brush! Scrub-a scrub scrub! You're a strange little thing, but I could use your help."

And so Thumbelina stayed with the field mouse in the warmth. She tidied and polished, swept and sang. Mrs. Mouse had saved her life, and Thumbelina felt she would do anything to repay her.

Then one day, Mrs. Mouse invited Mr. Mole to visit. She and Thumbelina cleaned all day until the house was spick as spit and spot as span. Mrs. Mouse was very excited for him to arrive.

"You'll love Mr. Mole! He's magnificent! He carries a book! He has a gold watch! You must dance for him! Wait, no. He's a bit blind. You must dance and sing!"

Bang, bang!

"Ooooh! That's him!"

Mrs. Mouse went to the back door that led to a dark passage Thumbelina had never explored. Mr. Mole stepped in out of the darkness. He was dressed in black velvet.

"This is Thumbelina. She can cook and clean, and she's clever! She can probably read to you. She's such a good little helper!"

Mr. Mole sniffed the air, peered up and down, scuffled noisily around Thumbelina and then stood squinting at her like a quiet question.

"There's honey and thistledown, nuts and berries. Sit here by the fire!" squeaked Mrs. Mouse.

"Dance!" said Mr. Mole so suddenly that Mrs. Mouse rattled the china. Thumbelina didn't want to dance. But not to disappoint Mrs. Mouse, she began to move her feet up and down.

I am Thumb, I am Thumble, I'm Thumbelina!
I sweep and I step to the beat,
Outside it is hushed,
So I tidy and brush,
Now the sun has forgotten the wheat.

Mr. Mole spoke up. "Come and live in my house. It's dark, but I have lots of room. You can stay as long as you like. I'll take you there now."

Mrs. Mouse threw up her hands in triumph and scampered in an excited circle. "Yes, yes!" she cried. "My little home is much too small to share with you forever. You shall live with Mr. Mole."

Mr. Mole lit a firebrand and shuffled into the dark passageway. "Follow me!"

"I don't want to live with him!" whispered Thumbelina to Mrs. Mouse. "I don't want to live in the dark forever." But Mrs. Mouse pushed her into the tunnel as if she couldn't hear.

The Injured Sparrow

The passage was damp and cold. Halfway along they came to a dead swallow. His wing was at a strange angle, and his feathers were dull. He lay stiff and still. Thumbelina began to cry silently. Mr. Mole kicked the swallow with a club claw.

"Ugh, birds!" he spat. "Such a load of work filling up the hole he left. He dropped down from the sky and fell through my earth. But soon he'll be nothing but dust!"

Thumbelina didn't really look at Mr. Mole's house, although she was aware it was big and full of shiny, showy things. Mrs. Mouse twitched and pointed and pulled at her clothes, but Thumbelina's head was so dizzy that all she could hear were her own worries beating about in her brain.

Live with Mr. Mole? Live in the dark forever? Never! But then, where else will I go? . . . Poor swallow, so cold! Can he really be dead? I saw him swoop and heard his song all summer long.

That night Thumbelina couldn't sleep, and so she got up and wove a blanket out of straw. She took it to the swallow and laid it over his frozen wings. She hugged his neck, then lay down with him and put her head on the soft feathers of his chest.

"I'm sorry it's like this. Thank you for singing all summer," she whispered.

And then she jumped. *Thud, thud.* Something was beating in her ear. *Thud, thud.*

It was the swallow's heart! He was alive!

Thumbelina ran and brought leaves, hay — whatever she could to keep him warm. In secret, every night, she brought him rainwater in petals, and nuts and seeds on leaves. She looked after him all winter. In the dark passageway they swapped stories. The swallow remembered catching his wing on a thorn bush when flying south. He must have fallen because the next

thing he knew, he was in the passageway with Thumbelina leaning on his chest.

"Come away with me," he begged when she told him how she must move into Mr. Mole's dark house.

"I can't. I owe Mrs. Mouse my life. How will they manage without my help?"

By the time spring came, the swallow had fully recovered. One night, Thumbelina scrabbled and the swallow pecked the earth to open up a hole in the passageway.

"Fly!" said Thumbelina.

"Come with me!" begged the swallow. "I'll carry you with me on my back and take you to the sun!"

"I can't!"

Reluctantly, the swallow left at first light, but as the sun rose he couldn't help singing.

Thumbelina watched the empty, bright, wide blue sky for a long time.

CHAPTER SIX

Return to the Sunlight

Some days later, Mr. Mole blocked up the hole in the passage completely.

Thumbelina spent her time spinning and weaving a rug for Mr. Mole. She gently spooled the silk around a twig as a kind spider spun it out for her. And day and night Mrs. Mouse kept watch, brimming with excitement, humming a little tune, "Spin the thread, snip the thread, weave it and sew, when it is done, Thumbelina must go."

Then she added with a shrill laugh, "But not too far away! You'll still be here under the ground, Thumbelina!" Mrs. Mouse smiled at the small girl with her beady eyes.

Every night Mr. Mole came and sat by Mrs. Mouse's fire, pawing his golden watch, peering at Thumbelina and moaning. "I hate summer.

When the winter comes and shadows reign, I won't be alone anymore. Your little silk rug will look so lovely in our fine home."

In this way the warm, bright days passed in darkness. Thumbelina kept quiet, but her mind worked day and night, trying to think of a way out. She didn't know how she'd ever get back home to Mother. Only on the morning of her move to Mr. Mole's house did Thumbelina try to speak to Mrs. Mouse. "Thank you for everything you've done for me, but I don't want to live with Mr. Mole. We are very different creatures. Couldn't I stay here with you?"

With a whirl of a crisp apron, Mrs. Mouse turned on Thumbelina. Baring a set of fierce, sharp, white teeth she said, "No! Enough or I'll bite you! He'll be here in ten minutes." And off she bustled. Thumbelina bit back her tears.

As soon as Mrs. Mouse turned her back, Thumbelina ran to the door. She needed to look at the light. The wheat was so gold. It smelled of sunshine. Thumbelina ran in between the stalks. She had to say goodbye to the sky. In a clearing she threw her head back and began to sing.

I am Thumb,

I am Thumble,

I'm Thumbelina!

She had hardly begun when she heard an answering cry. A flock of swallows were flying south, ahead of the winter. One swallow separated from the flock and swooped towards her. "Thumbelina! We're going to the sun! Leave the cold and jump on my back."

It was her swallow!

Thumbelina thought of the bumpy toad. She thought of the buzzing beetle. And then she thought of Mother.

Thumbelina jumped.

With her arms around his neck and her feet in his feathers they began to fly, low at first, above wheat field and forest, then curving downriver to the stream. It seemed so far to Thumbelina!

The swallow took Thumbelina high, higher, above snowy mountains and wild seas. On and on they flew until Thumbelina smelled sweet orange, sharp lemon and fragrant herbs.

At first light, the swallow began to lose height. In loop after loop they soared towards land, and with each loop the air glimmered more brightly. When they finally hit grass, they were beside a daisy. As the morning sun rose, its white petals opened to reveal a tiny young man. He was only the tip of a fingernail taller than Thumbelina, with lacy wings as light as spun glass and a crown of golden pollen.

"Where are we?" Thumbelina asked the swallow.

"I have looped us into Faeryland," replied the bird, "and this is the king of the faeries. I think he might be able to help you find your way back to your home."

"So pleased to meet you!" Thumbelina smiled the widest of smiles.

The swallow began to twitter, telling the king their whole story. When he had finished, Thumbelina asked the king, "What's your name?"

With a burst of laughter, the young man began to spiral energetically up into the air.

I am Tan, I am Tino, I'm Tan Tantino!
I flit like a bird or a bee,
We could wing, skit and scud,
Between flower and bud,
If you wanted to join up with me?

"Yes!" Thumbelina shouted, kicking her heels and somersaulting as the swallow swooped around them in lazy circles of joy. "I want to go home to my mother!"

"Then you'll be needing wings," said Tantino. He whistled, and in a shimmer the air was alive with fluttering. Damselflies, dragonflies and mayflies surrounded them. They gave Thumbelina a pair of shining wings. Breathless with joy, she sewed them to her dress using the spine of a thistle and thread from a spider. Tantino stared. "You're very clever," he said. "Would you show me how to sew?"

Thumbelina smiled. "Of course! If you show me how to make a crown!"

Tantino darted and scooped handfuls of sticky flower pollen to fashion a crown for Thumbelina. When he put the gold on her head, she did a back flip and the crown flew off. Tantino caught it and they fell about laughing.

"Let's go!" said Thumbelina. And so, with a flit and a loop, a skit and a swoop they were up and away, and when they arrived at Mother's house, there was no doubt that they'd fallen in love.

By and by, Thumbelina and Tantino had as many children as there are stars in the sky, so that every flower in the world became a home to tiny dancing faeries. Thumbelina's mother spent the rest of her days surrounded by her little faery grandchildren.

You may catch a glimpse of them if you're up early on May's Eve or Midsummer's Day, when the veil between our world and the world of the faeries is thin. You'll spot them the second the flowers unfurl in the sun.

And then they're gone.